Waltham Forest Libraries

Please return this item by the last date stamped. The loan may be renewed unless required by another customer.

10/2020

D1586250

Need to renew your books?
http://www.walthamforest.gov.uk/libraries or
Dial 0333 370 4700 for Callpoint – our 24/7 automated telephone renewal line. You will need your library card number and your PIN. If you do not know your PIN, contact your local library.

Meet the Ballet Bunnies

Dolly

You'll never meet a bunny who loves to dance as much as Dolly.

Fifi

If you're in trouble, Fifi is always ready to lend a helping paw!

Pod

Pod loves to build things out of the bits and bobs he finds. He also loves his tutu!

Trixie

Yawn! When she's not dancing, Trixie likes curling up and having a nice snooze.

Great Clarendon Street, Oxford OX2 6DP

Oxford University Press is a department of the University of Oxford.
It furthers the University's objective of excellence in research, scholarship,
and education by publishing worldwide. Oxford is a registered trade mark
of Oxford University Press in the UK and in certain other countries

Ballet Bunnies

Let's Dance

By Swapna Reddy

Illustrated by Binny Talib

OXFORD
UNIVERSITY PRESS

Chapter 1

Miss Luisa's School of Dance
was curiously noisy when Millie turned
up for her ballet lesson. The usual buzz
of students hurrying to lessons and the
plinking of the piano in the nearby studio
were today drowned out by overexcited
children shouting to be heard.

Millie squeezed through the crowd gathered in the hallway and headed for the studio ahead of her classmates. She checked that no one had noticed her

before she hurried inside and over to the curtained stage. She knew exactly who could tell her what was going on at Miss Luisa's School of Dance.

'Millie!' Fifi squealed as Millie clambered on to the stage and scooped up the tiny bunny hopping towards her.

The rest of the Ballet Bunnies—Dolly, Pod, and Trixie—were all sitting finishing off their breakfast by an upturned teacup table.

'What's going on?' Millie asked, turning and pointing at the crowded hallway.

'Isn't it thrilling?' Dolly cried. She pirouetted towards Millie. 'There's going to be a gala performance!'

Millie looked confused. True, in front
of her were four *talking* bunnies —well,
three talking bunnies to be accurate, as
Trixie had balled herself up amongst the
soft fabric of a discarded tutu and

was snoring gently—

but it wasn't the bunnies that confused Millie.

'What's a gala performance?' she asked.

'Dolly!' Pod tutted, pulling on his long ears. 'I thought we weren't going to say anything until Millie heard the news from Miss Luisa.'

'I don't care. I'm too excited!' Dolly danced in circles and then grabbed Pod's paw and spun him towards Millie. 'The gala performance is *only* the biggest ballet show of the year!' she exclaimed. 'Everyone at Miss Luisa's School of Dance is involved!'

'Including you, Millie,' Fifi said, nudging her, then jumping down to join Pod and Dolly.

A wide grin stretched across Millie's face.

'I'll be dancing on stage?' she said. 'In front of a proper audience—like a proper ballet dancer?'

Fifi and Dolly nodded excitedly, while Pod peered around the curtain at the studio.

'Millie, quick!' he whispered. 'Your class is about to start!'

Chapter 2

'We're going to be in a show!'
Samira screeched, as soon as she spotted
Millie.

'I know!' Millie shrieked back at her
friend.

'How did you find out?' Samira said.
'I was looking for you in the hallway

when Miss Luisa revealed the surprise,
but I didn't see you.'

'Oh, I heard it from a little bunny,'
Millie said, fiddling with the hem of
her tutu.

'You are silly, Millie.' Samira smiled and shook her head.

'Well, you haven't heard *everything*,' their classmate Amber said smugly, joining the duo. 'We're going to be dancing with props.' She glared down her nose at Millie. '*I* know because *my* mum has arranged it all.'

Before any of the girls could say anything further, Miss Luisa tapped the wooden barre beam, calling the class to attention.

'As I said earlier,' she said, 'this year's theme will be "The Garden".'

Samira grabbed Millie's arm, and

they grinned at each other.

'The oldest students will be our swans, the minis will be the seedlings, and you will all be the flower fairies,' Miss Luisa explained.

The entire class took a huge breath. Flower fairies! Even Amber managed an excited smile at Millie before remembering they weren't friends and dropping her beam to a frown.

'All of us, Miss Luisa?' she asked. 'Some of us haven't been dancing quite as long as the others, and I'm worried they'll let the performance down.' She looked deliberately at Millie so that everyone knew exactly who she was talking about.

'Yes, Amber,' Miss Luisa replied. 'The whole class will be performing together, so you must work as a team.'

Chapter 3

Miss Luisa pointed to a box in the corner of the studio.

'You will all take a watering can from the box. You must not lose it, so please remember which can is yours.'

Millie rushed to her feet as everyone charged over to the box to pick their

favourite colours.
As Millie reached
down for the blue
can, Amber snatched
it out of her hands.

'But you already have the pink one,'
Millie said, staring at the two watering
cans in Amber's hands.

'Well, now I want the blue,' snapped
Amber, dropping the pink watering can
so that it clattered on the wooden floor.

'Be careful with your props,' Miss
Luisa tutted, as Millie picked up the
abandoned watering can.

Millie hugged the pink watering can

close to her chest and carried it over to the middle of the studio to join her class. She didn't mind all that much that it wasn't the blue can—she was too excited about the show. Not even Amber could bring her down today. Besides, pink was one of her favourite colours too.

'First we will practise without the
props,' instructed Miss Luisa.

She talked the class through the
ballet routine, and Millie, who had been

dancing for a few weeks now, found
herself picking up the steps quickly.
She had a bunny or four to thank for
the extra lessons she'd had.

But as soon as the students picked up their props, they all forgot their steps and soon found themselves in a knot of arms, legs, and cans. Even Will, the best dancer in the class, dropped his watering can a few times.

'It's a good thing there's no water in this,' Samira said, as she untangled her arms from Millie's and sent her watering can crashing to the floor for the millionth time.

'Samira, please remember you are a flower fairy, not a frog,' Miss Luisa said, straightening up Samira's back. 'I want to see graceful and light footwork.'

Samira swung her watering can out

and pirouetted straight into the barre.
She collapsed in a heap on the floor
before pretending to take a long drink
from the spout of her
watering can. Even
Miss Luisa was in fits
of giggles.

'At least be a graceful frog,' she said, laughing and pulling Samira to her feet.

By the end of the lesson, Millie had to admit she was proud of herself and the rest of the class. They had worked hard together and looked like a proper ballet troupe—even Millie and Amber had managed to steer clear of each other and avoid an argument.

As an end-of-class treat, Miss Luisa showed them their costumes for the show. The girls each had a tutu made up of fabric petals that matched the colour of their watering cans. And the boys got to choose their tights and leotard sets, each embellished with a cascade of delicately sewn flowers. Millie ran her hand over the velvet-soft petals on her pink tutu. She couldn't wait for the gala performance.

Chapter 4

Millie spent the entire week
rehearsing as much as she could. She
tottered around the house with her
watering can. She practised in the park.
She spun around the dinner table. Even
at bedtime, when her feet ached and
she couldn't stifle the yawns, she made

herself lift up her chin and stretch her neck. She was determined to be the most graceful flower fairy at Miss Luisa's School of Dance.

On the day of the dress rehearsal, Millie made sure she was the first to arrive at the school—not just to pick up her costume, but to tell the Ballet Bunnies how hard she had been working on the routine.

'Please take us to the theatre with you,' Fifi said, as Millie gathered her up with the rest of the bunnies in a ginormous hug. 'We can come to the dress rehearsal, stay over, and be ready for the real performance!'

'By bunny fluff, you must!' Dolly insisted. 'Last time we travelled to the

theatre, we had to hide in the box of spare ballet slippers and Trixie kept disappearing into the shoes.'

'Will you be OK staying overnight at the theatre?' Millie asked.

'Of course!' said Pod. 'We wouldn't want to miss your big moment.'

'We've packed our overnight bags,' Trixie added.

There, stacked neatly in a row, were four tiny squares of silk which had been rolled up and pinned to make bunny-sized sleeping bags.

Millie opened her rucksack, and Fifi, Dolly, Pod, and Trixie hopped in with

their packs. Holding her costume, she carefully carried her friends on her back to the bus, where Samira had saved a seat for her.

The theatre was a short drive from the school, and, as the bus pulled up, Millie felt the bubble of excitement in

her belly grow. Both she and Samira had been humming the flower fairy song all the way to the theatre, but they both fell silent as the bus pulled up by the grand columned entrance, with its paved marble tiles and its huge oak doors with twirly golden handles.

Miss Luisa got out first to pull open the theatre doors, and the children filed in behind in pairs through the long red-carpeted lobby.

'Off you go,' Millie whispered to the bunnies, as she dropped to the floor, pretending to tie her shoelaces.

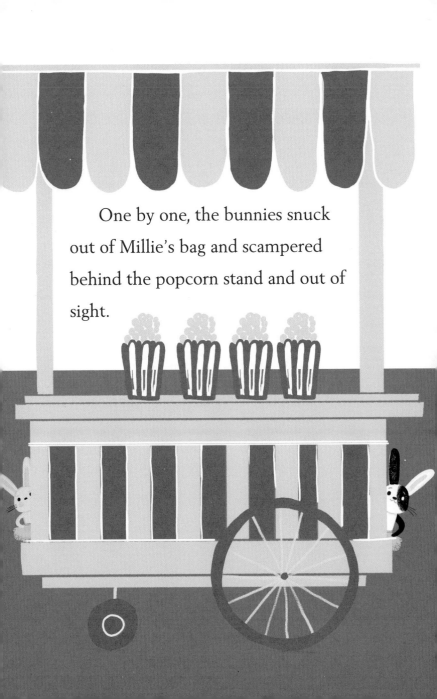

One by one, the bunnies snuck out of Millie's bag and scampered behind the popcorn stand and out of sight.

Millie followed her classmates through the lobby and into the theatre hall. Rows and rows of red velvet seats lined the hall—all the way from the front of the stage to the doors at the back of the room. As Millie looked up at the intricately painted ceiling, she could also see seats at different levels reaching high up to the top.

Come performance night, each of the many seats would be filled. And each and every person in those seats would be watching Millie.

Chapter 5

The children climbed

onstage and split off into their groups.
The older students left to practise
offstage, while Millie's class and the minis
were guided to the dressing rooms to try
on their costumes.

Millie got ready quickly then stood

on the stage and looked out at the sea of chairs. The excited bubble in her tummy was disappearing fast, and a swirl of knots

was growing instead. As Miss Luisa called her class to rehearse, Millie's throat was dry and her feet seemed frozen to the

floor like solid ice blocks.

'What are you doing?' Amber hissed at her. 'Miss Luisa has called us.'

Millie opened her mouth to reply, but the words did not come. As the flower fairies song started to boom from the speakers, Millie found herself forcing her legs to move in time with her classmates—but she was concentrating so hard on not dropping her watering can that she was in plié when she should have been in relevé and in relevé when she should have been in plié.

'Millie,' Miss Luisa said, gently. 'Why don't we take a break and practise offstage for a while?'

Millie nodded and ran as
fast as she could away from
the stage and the rows and rows
of seats.

Samira followed her. 'Wait for me,'
she whispered nervously behind Millie.
But before Millie could say a word,
the rest of their class had joined them.

'You better not mess up like
that on the night,' Amber snarled.
'You're going to make us *all* look
bad.'

Millie looked down. Her stomach
churned. She didn't want to make anyone
look bad. What was she going to do?

Chapter 6

As the minis took to the stage to rehearse their seedling routine, Millie changed out of her costume, found a quiet corner behind the curtains, and hid from her class.

She had rehearsed *all* week. She knew the routine off by heart. She could probably perform it in her sleep! But when she looked out at the rows of seats and imagined them filled with hundreds of people, her feet refused to move.

'Millie?' a tiny voice called.

Millie looked down and recognized Dolly's familiar silky coat.

'Oh, Dolly,' she said, relieved. 'I'm so glad you're here.'

'Come on,' Dolly said. 'I'll show you where we've set up camp.'

Millie followed Dolly around the back of the stage towards a set of shelves. The bunnies had made themselves at home. A small thread of fairy lights lit up a cosy nook, which was lined with soft silk and velvet from a discarded costume and furnished with two popcorn trays for beds.

'Didn't Pod do well?' Fifi said, as Millie peered in at their hideaway.

'He certainly did,' Millie said, smiling at the clever bunny.

On another shelf, Millie saw

that the rest of the silk and velvet had been used to create curtains, which had been tied back with gold ribbon from the tops of the confectionery bags being sold in the lobby.

'What's this?' Millie asked.

Fifi jumped down and into the shelf. She pirouetted between the curtains and leapt high before landing in a curtsy. 'This is *our* theatre,' she said, with a bow. 'We're putting on our own ballet show tonight for the theatre mice, and they're going to perform a play for us!'

'That sounds brilliant!' Millie exclaimed. 'I wish I could see it.'

'Our gala performance is called "The Ballet Bunny Garden" and we're all going to be Ballet Bunny flower fairies,' Fifi explained.

'I'm going to be the pink one, just like you, Millie,' Dolly added, holding up a pink cupcake case that she had turned into a tutu.

Millie grinned, but her smile soon
disappeared when Dolly asked about
her rehearsal.

'I don't know what happened,'
she said sadly. 'I rehearsed non-stop all
week, but it all went wrong today. I'm so
worried about making a mistake that it's
making me make lots of mistakes!'

'Oh, Millie, you're nervous about
performing on stage,' Fifi said, gently.

'I understand, Millie,' Dolly said.
'I feel the same way about dancing for
the mice. I'm worried I'll forget my
steps too.'

'But you're so brilliant, Dolly!' Millie
said. 'You have nothing to be nervous
about. You always look like you are
having so much fun when you're dancing.

Even if you *do* make a mistake, no one
will notice because they'll be having so
much fun with you.'

Dolly smiled at Millie. 'You're right,'
she said slowly. 'I can only do my best.
I should just try and enjoy it and stop
worrying quite so much.'

'Exactly,' Fifi
agreed, nodding
along, and then she,
Dolly, and Pod smiled
up at Millie.

Millie smiled
back. Even if *she*
made a small mistake,

everyone would see how much she loved dancing too.

Why hadn't she told herself that earlier?

Chapter 7

'Are you ready, Millie?'
Trixie asked, joining Dolly and Fifi.

'I think so.' Millie picked up Trixie and nuzzled her soft fur against her cheek.

'When I'm nervous, I take some deep breaths in and out, and it helps me calm down,' Trixie said. 'I can show you if you want.'

'Yes please,' Millie replied.

She sat on the floor, and Trixie and the other three bunnies joined her.

'Everyone shut your eyes,' Trixie told them.

Millie and the bunnies closed their eyes obediently.

'Now breathe in,' Trixie said.

They all inhaled.

'And breathe out,' she said, nodding as they exhaled their deep breaths.

'In.'

'Out.'

'In.'

'Out.'

'Zzzzzzzz.'

Millie opened her eyes to find that
Trixie's calming breaths had put the
tiniest of the bunnies right back to sleep.
Pod giggled, and Fifi had to put a paw
over his mouth to stop him from waking
Trixie, while Millie picked her up and
gently placed her in a popcorn-tray bed.

'Bunny fluff!' Fifi exclaimed. 'I've just had an idea!'

She hopped towards Millie's watering can and jumped straight in.

Millie peered in, and the little bunny peered back up, her eyes shiny with excitement.

'Dolly could be inside your watering can while you dance, and that way you won't be alone,' Fifi said. 'She'll remind you to have fun!' The little bunny spun a pirouette inside the can. 'Pod could make a little seat from some of the old programmes, and it will be just like being on a ride at the fair.'

Dolly leapt up and down as she and
Millie squealed with glee at the idea of
being on stage together in the show.

Chapter 8

Performance night had arrived, and Miss Luisa was wandering around backstage checking costumes and props whilst the students slipped on their ballet shoes and talked through their routines excitedly. The noise in the theatre hall was building as families and friends filled the rows and rows of seats.

Millie smoothed down the petals of her tutu and patted her hair, which Mum had pulled up into a neat bun high on her head. Mum had even added some sparkles to Millie's cheeks before wishing her luck and heading into the hall to find a front-row seat.

'Please leave your props at the side of the stage,' Miss Luisa called out. 'And good luck, everyone,' she said, giving them all a huge thumbs up.

Millie squinted to look inside her watering can. Dolly was sitting there, strapped in tight to a padded seat that Pod had made from some old programmes and a ticket book.

'Are you OK in there?' Millie asked.

'Yes.' Dolly looked up with a big grin. 'Are you OK out there?'

Millie tried to nod, but her tummy felt like it had a flock of butterflies inside it, trying hard to escape.

'Let's try Trixie's calming breaths,' Dolly said.

They breathed in and out and in and out again. With every breath, Millie felt the churning feeling in her tummy lessen, as though she was blowing out the butterflies with each lungful.

She placed the watering can down with the other props and gave Dolly a tiny kiss on her head before taking her place next to Samira and watching as the curtains came apart.

The gala performance was
about to begin.

Chapter 9

'Flower fairies,' Miss Luisa whispered to the children. 'You're up next!'

Millie tore her eyes away from the older students, who were halfway through their swan dance. She rushed off towards the props to find her watering can and Dolly.

'Good luck, Millie,' Samira said, as she hurried past with her own can. 'See you up there!'

'Good luck, Samira,' Millie whispered back excitedly.

She reached the side of the stage and looked for her pink can. It wasn't there. It wasn't where she'd left it. She checked behind the curtain, under the table, and in the boxes. She searched amongst the rucksacks and lunch boxes. It had completely disappeared.

'Oh no. Oh no. Oh no,' she whispered, panicked.

'What's wrong, Millie?'
Fifi asked, hopping over with Pod
and Trixie. 'We just came to wish
you and Dolly good luck.'

'My watering can has gone!'
Millie said, hunting through the
folds of the curtain
again. 'And Dolly's
inside.'

Her hands shook as she shoved her way through boxes of costumes, dumping them on to their sides, searching for the little bunny.

Millie suddenly stopped. There on the floor, where her watering can had been, was a blue petal. A blue petal from a blue flower tutu.

'Amber!' Millie cried. 'Amber must've taken the can, and Dolly too.'

'Don't worry, Millie,' Fifi reassured her. 'Dolly's made of tough bunny fluff. We'll find her.'

Catching Dolly's scent, the bunnies dashed off behind the stage. Millie sprinted after them.

'She's here somewhere!' Pod said, his long ears twitching. 'I can hear her!'

'I can't hear anything,' Millie said, as the swan song blared loudly backstage.

'She's definitely here,' Pod said. 'I can hear her thumping her feet.'

'In here!' Fifi shouted, jumping up and down by a closed bin. 'I think Dolly's in here.'

Millie yanked off the lid. There, inside the dark bin, was her pink watering can and an agitated but safe Dolly.

Millie lifted Dolly out of the can and hugged her close.

'Are you OK?' Millie asked.

'I'm fine,' Dolly huffed. 'That Amber took our can and dumped it in the bin.'

'I thought so,' replied Millie, before telling her about the blue petal.

'I could've climbed out, but the bin lid was too heavy,' Dolly said. 'Thankfully

Amber didn't
see me.'

The last few lines of the swan song
played. There were only a few seconds

left before Millie had to be on stage.

'I think we have a show to do,' Dolly said, hearing the music die down.

She jumped out of Millie's hands and back into the can.

'Are you sure?' Millie asked.

'By bunny fluff, I am!' Dolly grinned. 'Not even Amber can ruin our fun tonight.'

Chapter 10

'There you are!' Samira said, as Millie skidded to a stop by her friend. 'We're on!'

The music began to crescendo, and the flower fairies took to the stage. A feeling of calm came over Millie when she spotted Mum in the front row,

whooping for her louder than anyone
else in the audience.

Millie felt her body rock and sway to
the music as she bobbed up and down
in time with the others. She had been so
busy trying to find Dolly backstage that
she hadn't had time to feel nervous. With

Dolly cheering her on the whole way through the performance, by the time the song ended Millie just wanted it to start all over again so she could dance some more.

The crowd were on their feet as
Millie and her class curtsied and bowed.
The sea of seats was now an ocean of
smiles. Samira grabbed Millie's hand,
and she and Millie took another curtsy as
the crowd cheered even louder. Out of

the corner of her eye, Millie
spotted Amber stomping off, but that
wasn't going to ruin her night.

She stuck out her chin and thrust
her shoulders back before taking a final
curtsy. As she lowered her head, she
spotted Dolly beaming up at her with
pride.

'You did it!' the little bunny mouthed proudly.

Millie's heart felt so full. She couldn't wait for the gala performance next year.

Basic ballet moves

First position

Second position

Third
position

Fourth
position

Fifth position

Glossary of ballet terms

Barre – A horizontal bar at waist level on which ballet dancers rest a hand for support during certain exercises.

Demi – A small bend of the knees, with heels kept on the floor.

En pointe – Dancing on the very tips of your toes.

Grand – A large bend of the knees, with heels raised off the floor.

Pas de deux – A dance for two people.

Pirouette – A spin made on one foot, turning all the way round.

Plié – A movement in which a dancer bends the knees and straightens them again, while feet are turned out and heels are kept on the floor.

Relevé – A movement in which the dancer rises on the tips of the toes.

Sauté – A jump off both feet, landing in the same position.

About the author

Award-winning author Swapna Reddy, who also writes as Swapna Haddow, lives in New Zealand with her husband and son and their dog, Archie.

If she wasn't writing books, she would love to run a detective agency or wash windows because she's very nosy.

About the illustrator

Binny Talib is a Sydney based illustrator who loves to create wallpaper, branding, children's books, editorial, packaging and anything else she can draw all over.

Binny recently returned from living in awesome Hong Kong and now works happily on beautiful Sydney harbour with other lovely creative folks, drinking copious amounts of dandelion tea, and is inspired by Jasper her rescue cat.

If you enjoyed this adventure, you might also like . . .